SANTA'S WISH

Written by **Kristina Rowlands**

Illustrated by **Mia Lloyd**

For the Magic of Christmas

For finding your way back through the darkness each year,
Spreading kindness, joy and Christmas cheer.

Published in association with Bear With Us Productions

ISBN 978-1-9196413-2-4

SANTA'S WISH

Written by **Kristina Rowlands**

Illustrated by **Mia Lloyd**

Christmas is a magical time,
with Christmas carols, stories
and rhymes.

Writing to Father Christmas takes some thinking,

while the stars in the sky are all twinkling.

Getting the food ready on time,

while the decorations all
sparkle and shine.

Remember to get a treat for Santa and his reindeer friends,

they have a lot to do before Christmas night ends.

santa and his helpers are very busy,
running around until they're dizzy.

They're trying to work as **fast** as they can,
to make sure everything's going to **plan**.

We watch children in a Nativity play,
who've practised hard for the right words to say.

There's lots of fun at the Christmas fair,
where we decorate gingerbreads to share.

It's been getting colder every day,
snow has even come our way!

We build a **snowman** and have lots of fun,

and go on a thrilling **toboggan** run.

When we're feeling cold and starting to tire,
we warm up in front of the fire.

We drink hot chocolate with marshmallows in,
while waiting for more fun to begin.

As we settle down
next to our tree,

Santa is hoping
we feel as happy
as can be.

With family, friends
and lots of **fun**,

the Christmas spirit is
enjoyed by **everyone**.

Santa is wishing for his
dream to come true,

for everyone to feel
safe and included too.

For little acts of kindness to last through the year,

not just when Christmas is near.

And if **everyone** can look after
the world with great care,

We can **all** live happily
together there.

So, when you're putting
up your stocking tonight,

remember to listen
out into the night...

To see if you might be able to hear,
Santa humming a song as he gets near.

Children are waiting patiently everywhere,
for Santa's sleigh to fly through the air.

Finally, with Christmas lights
— oh so bright,
both big and small can find their
way home in the night.

Soon everyone will be fast **asleep**,
in the big forest, everything's
quiet **without** **a peep.**

And once **presents** are
delivered and **happiness** is spread,

Santa will fly back home to his bed.

Feeling happy that everything has been done,

he will wish a Merry Christmas to everyone!

Made in the USA
Middletown, DE
31 August 2023

37659236R00018